MARC

D0462231

ARTHUR IN A PICKLE

Step into Reading® Sticker Books

Random House 🏠 New York

www.randomhouse.com/kids

Library of Congress Cataloging-in-Publication Data
Brown, Marc Tolon. Arthur in a pickle / [text and illustrations by] Marc Brown. p. cm.
SUMMARY: After lying about what happened to his homework, Arthur has such
a bad dream about being "in a pickle" that he decides to tell the truth.
ISBN 0-679-88469-6 (trade) — ISBN 0-679-98469-0 (lib. bdg.)
[1. Aardvark—Fiction. 2. Homework—Fiction. 3. Honesty—Fiction. 4. Pickles—Fiction.]
I. Title. PZ7.B81618Aldi 1999 [E]—dc21 98-43340
Printed in the United States of America 10 9 8 7 6 5 4 3 2 1

STEP INTO READING is a registered trademark of Random House, Inc.

ARTHUR is a registered trademark of Marc Brown.

The school bell rang.
"Time to hand in your homework,"
said Mister Ratburn.
Everyone did—but Arthur.

"Where is your homework?"

Mister Ratburn asked Arthur.

"My dog ate it," said Arthur.

"I don't think so,"
said Mister Ratburn.
"Go to the principal's office
first thing in the morning.
You're in a pickle now, Arthur."

That night, Arthur just played
with his food.

He tossed and turned in bed.

"I'm in a pickle," he said again

and again until he fell asleep.

Arthur dreamed that the pickle police were chasing him!

8

He jumped into his pickle car.

He stepped on the gas—

but he didn't get far.

The pickle police said,

"Take him away!"

Up in the sky, a pickle plane
flew through pickle snow
and rain.

10

The pilot threw down a rope
and pulled Arthur up.

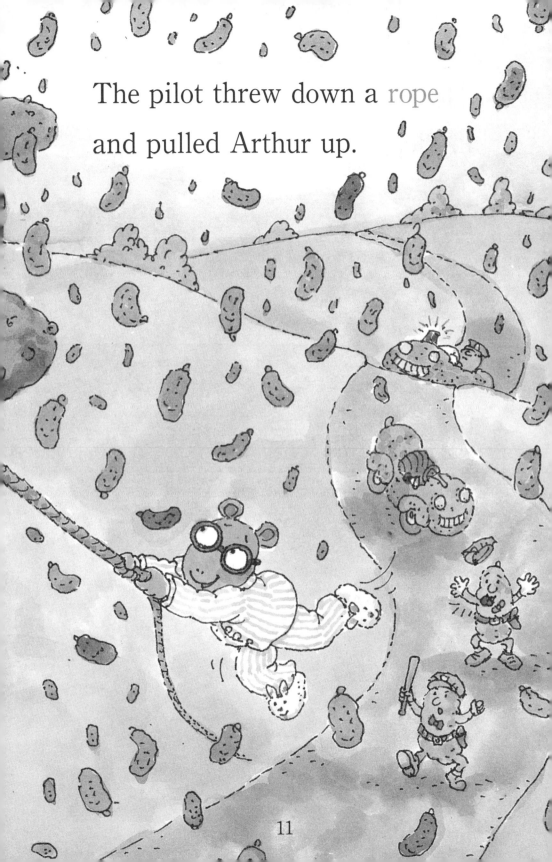

The plane went down
in Pickletown.

12

"Look!" said D.W. "A pickle steeple!"

"Look!" said Arthur. "Pickle people!"

13

Some had pickle hair.

Some had pickle toes.

Some a pickle ear.

Some a pickle nose.

"You're going to jail—
and absolutely no bail!"
shouted Judge Picklepuss.

The jailer put Arthur
on a pickle diet,
and every day he said,
"Just try it."

For breakfast, pickle doughnuts and pickle flakes . . .

For lunch, pickle pie and pickle shakes . . .

For dinner, pickle soup and pickle cakes.

"Let me out!

Don't be so mean.

I've had it," moaned Arthur.

"I'm turning green."

Suddenly, Arthur woke up.

He went to his desk,

opened his book,

and did his homework.

At school, Arthur went right
to the principal's office.
"I cannot tell a lie," he said.
"My dog did not eat
my homework.
I did not do my homework.
But here it is now.
I'm sorry."
The principal smiled.
"Well, thank you, Arthur,"
he said.

Arthur felt great all day—
until he asked,
"What's for dinner?"
and Dad said,
"Pickled cabbage!"